Yunmi and Halmoni's Trip

Sook Nyul Choi

Illustrated by Karen Dugan

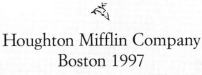

Houghton Mifflin Company
Boston 1997

Acknowledgements:

My sincere thanks to Audrey Bryant for her interest in my work and to Dr. Peter Netland for his encouragement.

My special thanks to the Korea Foundation for the research grant that helped me write this book.

Text copyright © 1997 by Sook Nyul Choi
Illustrations copyright © 1997 by Karen Dugan

For information about this and other Houghton Mifflin
trade and reference books and multimedia products, visit
The Bookstore at Houghton Mifflin on the World Wide
Web at http://www.hmco.com/trade/.

The text of this book is set in 15.5 Simoncini Garamond.
The illustrations are watercolor, reproduced in full color.

Library of Congress Cataloging-in-Publication Data

Choi, Sook Nyul.
    Yunmi and Halmoni's trip / by Sook Nyul Choi; illustrated by Karen
M. Dugan.
        p. cm.
    Summary: When she goes to Korea with her grandmother, Yunmi looks
forward to visiting relatives she has never seen, but she also worries about
whether Halmoni will want to return to New York.
    ISBN 0-395-81180-5
    [1. Korea — Fiction. 2. Korean Americans — Fiction.
3. Grandmothers — Fiction. 4. Family life — Korea — Fiction.]
    I. Dugan, Karen, ill. II. Title.
PZ7.C44626Yu 1997   96-22013
[E] — dc20   CIP
                          AC

Manufactured in the United States of America

BVG 10 9 8 7 6 5 4 3 2 1

For Audrey and Kathy
— S.N.C.

For Marguerite R. Davis & William Davis with love
— K.M.D.

Yunmi settled into the airplane seat and took her grandmother's hand. It was Yunmi's first airplane trip. Her Halmoni, or grandmother, had come from Korea to take care of Yunmi while her parents were at work. Now Halmoni was taking Yunmi for a visit to Korea to meet all her aunts and uncles and cousins. Halmoni also wanted Yunmi to join Grandfather's birthday celebration. Yunmi's grandfather had died many years before, but each year the whole family visited his grave and celebrated his birthday.

Yunmi was very excited. She had gotten her very first passport for this trip. And she had promised to send lots of postcards to her best friends Helen and Anna Marie. It was a long flight from New York City across the Pacific Ocean to Seoul. It would take fourteen and a half hours. Halmoni, however, had lots of things to talk about during their flight. She pulled out a thick bundle of photos of Yunmi's many relatives, and began to tell her about each of them. Halmoni said, "I think they will all be at Kimpo Airport. They are so excited to meet you and want to show you all around Seoul."

When the airplane landed, they hurried through the airport to have their passports checked.

Halmoni walked Yunmi over to the long line that said "Foreigners." The line moved slowly as the officer checked each passport. Halmoni got to stand in the fast-moving line that said "Nationals." Yunmi looked like all the Koreans in the nationals line, but she had to stand in the foreigners' line. It made her feel strange.

But when it was Yunmi's turn, the man checking passports smiled and said, "Welcome to Seoul. Are you here for a visit with your Halmoni?"

"Yes, how did you know?" asked Yunmi.

"I saw you talking with your Halmoni. She was my favorite high school teacher. I heard she went to America to be with her granddaughter. Please tell her Hojun said 'Welcome back.'"

Yunmi nodded happily. She wasn't a foreigner after all. People here already knew who she was. She was proud of Halmoni, too.

Halmoni was waiting for Yunmi, and they walked toward big sliding doors. Suddenly a huge crowd of people rushed toward them, waving and bowing. Yunmi stood still, her eyes wide. Everyone hugged her. Person after person bowed and embraced Halmoni. Halmoni was so happy, she had to wipe tears from her smiling face. Finally they walked past a long line of green and yellow taxis. An uncle ushered Halmoni and Yunmi into his car, and the rest of the relatives piled into cars and cabs.

They sped down broad highways, then through streets crowded with skyscrapers. In the middle of the city at the top of a narrow, winding street was a tall brick wall with a pretty iron gate. Inside was Halmoni's house. Halmoni's older sister, who lived there now, rushed out. A cat and a dog with a fluffy tail ran behind her. Halmoni embraced her sister and bent to pet her dog. "Oh, I missed you, too," she said to him. Then she lifted the cat onto her shoulder and carried her inside.

During the next several days, Yunmi's cousins
Jinhi and Sunhi took her sightseeing. They went to
the royal palace, called Kyong Bok Kung. Yunmi
liked running down the center of the wide steps,
where only the kings and queens and ministers had
once been allowed to walk.

They went to the bustling East Gate Market. A street vendor there was baking little cakes filled with sweet red beans. Jinhi, Sunhi, and Yunmi each bought one and ate the cakes as they roamed the crowded stalls. "Socks for sale," "Silk shirts here," "Parasols on special," the vendors chanted as the girls walked past. Then Yunmi's cousins took her to their favorite stall.

There, Yunmi bought two soft lavender and pink silk purses with shiny black tassels for her friends Anna Marie and Helen. Yunmi was having fun with her cousins, but it was a little hard to understand their English. And when Yunmi spoke Korean, her cousins giggled and said she sounded funny.

Yunmi had hardly seen Halmoni since they arrived. Her grandmother was often out, and when she was home, Yunmi's cousins always sat on her lap and got all her attention. "Halmoni, don't ever leave us again," they kept saying. Halmoni just smiled. Yunmi sometimes wished everyone would disappear so she and Halmoni could talk like they did in New York.

For the next few days, Halmoni did stay home. But all Yunmi's aunts and cousins came over to prepare for the big picnic at Grandfather's tomb. They spent two whole days in the kitchen, making marinated beef, vegetables, dumplings, and sweets. Halmoni rushed about, overseeing everything.

"Sunhi," Halmoni said as she gave her a hug, "why don't you be in charge of making the mandoo? You can teach Yunmi. The dumplings are her favorite."

Halmoni rushed back with stacks of thin white dumpling skins, a bowl of water, and a big bowl of meat-and-vegetable filling. Sunhi placed just the right amount of filling on half of a dumpling skin. Then she dipped her pinky in the water and ran it around half the edge of the mandoo skin. She folded it into a half-moon shape and pressed the edge shut. Yunmi tried making them too. Soon they started making funny-shaped mandoo. Some looked like round balls, others like little purses, and some just looked strange. Halmoni smiled as she hurried past.

Yunmi saw how happy Halmoni was with all her family, and Yunmi started to worry. What if Halmoni didn't want to leave? In New York, Halmoni had only Yunmi and her parents and Yunmi's friends. She was scared, but tried to think about how much Halmoni loved her.

The next day was Grandfather's birthday. They
loaded all the food and drink into big vans they
had rented. Everyone, all the cousins and uncles
and aunts, climbed in, and they sped toward the
outskirts of Seoul where Grandfather was buried.
As they rode through the big city streets and then
the winding country roads, Yunmi and her cousins
sang Korean songs, played cat's cradle, and folded
paper into the shapes of birds and baskets.

They stopped at the bottom of a small mountain.
Everyone got out and climbed all the way to the
top, to a small field. In the middle was a little hill
covered with soft green grass.

There on the hill was a large, flat stone with Grandfather's name on it. Below that were a lot of other names. Yunmi was surprised to see her parents' names and her name. Then she remembered Halmoni telling her it was a Korean custom to list the names of all the children and grandchildren on a tombstone. Yunmi went up and touched the cool stone and felt the warm sunlight on her hand. Meanwhile, Halmoni gathered the whole family. Together they made three deep bows to Grandfather.

Then Halmoni said, "Grandfather will be happy to see us all having a good time visiting him and each other on his birthday. Let's eat and celebrate this beautiful day." They sat down to a picnic with all the food they had prepared.

Yunmi had only been to a cemetery once before. She had seen people place flowers at a grave, say a prayer, and leave quietly. But in Korea, no one cried or looked sad. The cousins ran through the field collecting flowers and smooth stones for Grandfather's hill.

Yunmi wanted to talk with Halmoni, but everyone was crowded around her. Yunmi went and sat under a big tree all by herself to think. As she watched Halmoni, Yunmi grew more and more afraid that Halmoni would not want to go back to New York.

"Yunmi, help us look for more stones," said Sunhi.

"Why are you all by yourself?" Jinhi asked. "What's wrong?"

"Nothing. Nothing's wrong. Why don't you go sit with Halmoni. She's missed you all year," Yunmi said and burst into tears. She jumped up and ran, tears streaming down her cheeks.

When she couldn't run anymore, Yunmi threw herself on the grass and cried and cried. She imagined going back to New York all by herself, and all the lonely afternoons she would spend without Halmoni. She knew Halmoni was happy here, but it all seemed so unfair.

Soon she heard Halmoni's voice. "Yunmi, what's the matter?" She didn't answer.

Halmoni patted her. "Aren't you enjoying your visit? Everyone is so happy you're here. They wish you could stay longer."

Yunmi blurted, "They just want me to stay so they can keep you here. I know you want to stay. You're so happy and busy."

Halmoni sighed. "Oh, dear! Have I been that bad? I'm sorry. It's just that I want to take care of everything so I'll be ready to spend another year with you."

Yunmi looked up. "Another year with me?"

"Yes, Yunmi. Another year in New York, just as we planned."

Suddenly Yunmi felt ashamed and selfish. She stared down at the grass. "Halmoni, you have your house, your pets, and all your grandchildren and friends here. In New York, you only have my parents and me. If you want to stay, I understand."

Halmoni smiled. "I do miss everyone here, but I have a family I belong to in New York. And you have a family here too. We're lucky because we both have two families."

Yunmi thought of her cousins Sunhi and Jinhi. "Halmoni, I kept wishing all my cousins would disappear. They were so nice to me, and even helped me buy presents for my friends."

Halmoni stroked Yunmi's hair and said, "They like you so much, you are already one of their favorite cousins."

"Halmoni, do you think we can invite Jinhi and Sunhi to New York for a visit? I'd like to show them around," said Yunmi.

Halmoni smiled. "Oh, I know they would love to. Why don't you ask them?"

Yunmi heard her cousins calling. She took Halmoni's hand and helped her up. Together they walked over to join Yunmi's family.